THIS BOOK BELONGS TO:

_____

To:
Brayder
Be Awesome!
Love
Tammy J.

Words to Ponder Publishing Company, LLC
First Printing

This book is dedicated to all the boys and girls who are not afraid to always "do their very best" and to their caregivers who encourage, support, and motivate them towards success.

Never stop being your very best because "new cubs" move into your neighborhood. Who knows, maybe your very best will cause them to want to be their "very best" as well. - F.D.L.

Dedicated to my Dad.
We love and miss you. - M.W.

Being a well-behaved child and kind and compassionate adult is tested time and time again in our lives. Books can help support children in choosing good ways of behaving and being. Florenza Denise Lee has written a powerful children's book to do just that in *Barry Bear's Very Best: Learning to Say No to Negative Influences.* Beautifully illustrated by Michelle Wynn, this full-color book is the story of a young bear who chooses to be helpful and do his "very best". Yet, he's confronted by a group of new young bears who make negative choices. Barry has to make difficult decisions. Will he let the appropriate adults know? Will he choose to continue on a more positive path?

Young readers and parents might be a bit surprised by some of the choices the neighbor bears choose to make in the pages of *Barry Bear's Very Best,* but these are things that our children are confronted with regularly in their lives. Florenza Denise Lee is straightforward in making that clear. She doesn't hint around at what younger children may face regarding peer pressure or possibly even bullying. She drives home the point instead. But, Lee doesn't leave children wondering how to handle the situation. Instead, at the end of *Barry Bear's Very Best: Learning to Say No to Negative Influences,* she offers tips and advice on how to handle bullying for the victim, bystander and the bully. There can never be enough books on the market to help create positive change in the world, and Florenza Denise Lee's *Barry Bear's Very Best* is one every parent and child should read.

BARRY BEAR'S VERY BEST
Learning to Say *No* to *Negative Influences*

by *Florenza Denise Lee*
illustrated by *Michelle Wynn*

Meet Barry

Barry Bear is a very good bear
who strives to do his *very best.*

While in school, he listens to his teachers and always does *his very best*.

While home, Barry helps
Mother Bear by doing
his chores and always
does *his very best.*

Barry Bear is known in his neighborhood as a very helpful little bear who always does *his very best*.

Mother and Father tell Barry
Bear how proud they are of
how he strives to be *his very
best.* Hearing this makes
Barry very proud.

One day, a new family moves into Barry's neighborhood.

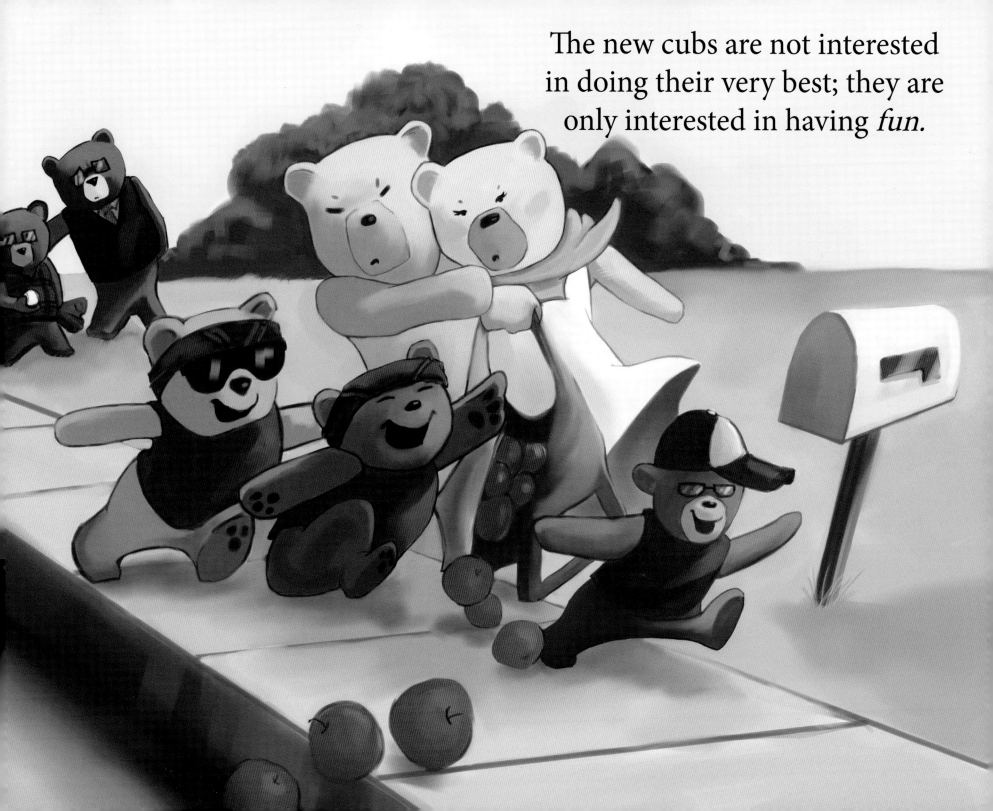

The new cubs are not interested in doing their very best; they are only interested in having *fun*.

When Barry walks to school, the cubs goof off and tease Barry for being a good bear.

While doing his chores, the cubs come along and try to prevent Barry from doing *his very best*.

No matter what Barry does, the cubs manage to be in his way.

One day, Barry Bear asks the new cubs if they would like to join him as he helps their neighbor; they laugh and say, "No way, we'd rather have *fun*!"

Even though they say, "No," Barry is happy he asked them to join him. He whistles as he helps their neighbor.

Barry tells Mother Bear about the cubs and she says, "Barry, you are a good bear, continue to do your very best and the very best will come your way."

One day, while on his way home from school, Barry notices that the cubs are drinking alcohol and smoking.

Barry tells Mother Bear right away. Mother is concerned and says she will speak with the cubs' mom. She then asks Barry to give her his paw.

Mother Bear traces his fingers and says, "Barry when you see someone using drugs or alcohol, I want you to pass by on the other side, and as you do, repeat these words:

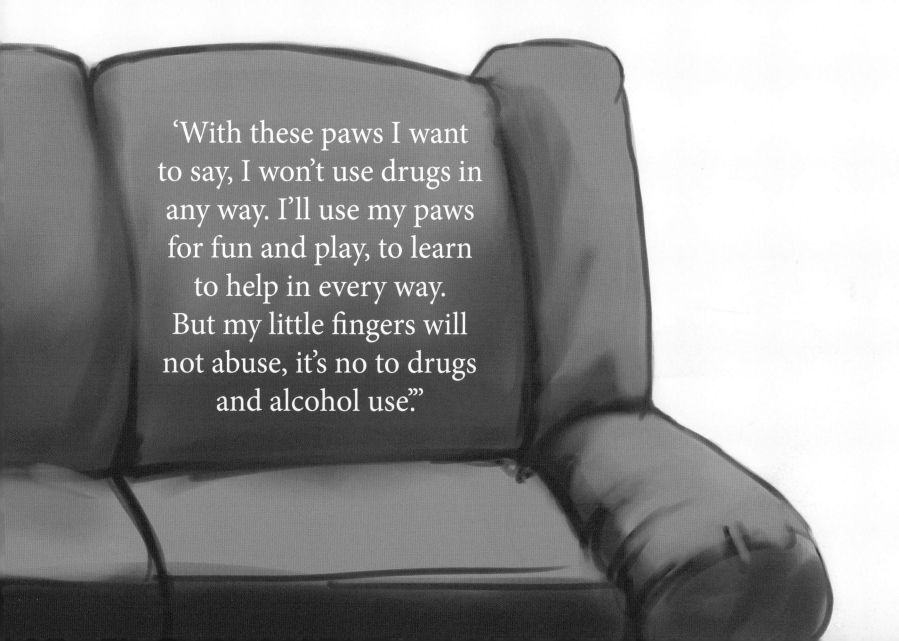

'With these paws I want to say, I won't use drugs in any way. I'll use my paws for fun and play, to learn to help in every way. But my little fingers will not abuse, it's no to drugs and alcohol use.'"

Mother Bear gives Barry a big hug then leaves to speak with the new cubs' mom.

When she returns, she checks in on Barry,

hears him repeating the words she had taught him, and smiles.

The next morning, Barry sees the cubs while on his way to school. He remembers the words Mother had taught him. As he passes by, he says to himself,

'With these paws I want
to say, I won't use drugs in
any way. I'll use my paws
for fun and play, to learn
to help in every way.
But my little fingers will
not abuse, it's no to drugs
and alcohol use."

Days turn into weeks, weeks
into months, months into
years, and as they do, Barry
continues to do *his very best.*

The day comes when Barry Bear becomes a Papa Bear with cubs of his own. Watching his children, Barry remembers the words his mother had once taught him.

Holding their paws, he says, "These are the words that Grandmother Bear once spoke to me, when I was a little cub like you.

Words that helped me
to become the bear I
am today. I want you to
remember these words
and use them often."

'With these paws I want
to say, I won't use drugs in
any way. I'll use my paws
for fun and play, to learn
to help in every way.
But my little fingers will
not abuse, it's no to drugs
and alcohol use."'

As Barry and his wife walk by the cubs' room, they overhear them repeating the words Barry taught them.

He looks at his wife and says, "We have the very best cubs ever."
"Indeed, we do," says Momma Bear, "Indeed, we do."

This checklist provides suggestions for what kids can do when bullying occurs –
written for students being bullied, students who witness bullying and the bullies themselves.

If you are bullied...

Reach Out

Tell an adult. Sometimes you may have to tell more than one trusted adult.

Ask your friends to help you. There is safety in numbers.

Practice what to say the next time you're bullied with your parents, teachers, or friends.

Be Cool in the Moment

Stay calm and confident. Don't show the bully that you're sad or mad.

Ignore the bully and walk away.

Remember: Fighting back can make bullying worse.

Change the School Community

Work with others to stop bully behavior; your whole school will benefit.

Remember: A lot of kids have to cope with bullying. You are not alone. No one deserves to be bullied.

If you witness bullying...

Interrupt It

Stand next to, or speak up for, the person being bullied.

Ask the bully to stop.

Comfort the person being bullied and offer friendship.

Get Help

Walk away and get help.

Find an adult who can intervene.

If you are the bully...

Make a Commitment to Change

Talk to an adult, like a teacher or parent, about how to get along with others.

Ask a friend to help you stop your bully behavior.

Apologize to the kids you have bullied.

Focus on Empathy and Responsibility
Think about what it feels like to be bullied -- would you want to be treated that way?

Before you speak, think about whether your words will help or hurt another student.

Change Your Behavior Resist peer pressure to bully.

If you start to bully, walk away and find something else to do.

Remember: You don't have to like everyone around you, but you have to treat everyone with respect.

Drawn from Stop Bullying Now, an initiative of the U.S. Department of Health and Human Services.